THIS WALKER BOOK BELONGS TO:

_____

_____

_____

_____

HETTY'S FIRST FLING

When the invitation to Great Uncle Fergus's seventy-fifth birthday party arrives, none of the Mungoe family is at all enthusiastic – except for Hetty. For although G.U.F. can be alarming and is only really interested in Little Highland Chiefs and not "wee girlies", to Hetty he is still a hero. What's more, the party is to take place far away on the Isle of Skye. Hetty's joy would be complete if only she could wear a kilt and butterfly tags like her brother James (who wishes just as much that he didn't have to wear them!). In the end, though, G.U.F.'s ceilidh turns out to be full of memorable surprises for everyone – and Hetty in particular.

WALKER STORYBOOKS

Earthquake by Ruskin Bond
Hetty's First Fling by Diana Hendry
Our Horrible Friend by Hannah Cole
Robin Hood and Little John
    by Julian Atterton
Robin Hood and the Miller's Son
    by Julian Atterton
The Shape-Changer by Julian Atterton
Staples for Amos by Alison Morgan
We Three Kings from Pepper Street Prime
    by Joan Smith

Hetty's First Fling

First published 1985 by
Julia MacRae Books
This edition published 1990 by
Walker Books Ltd, 87 Vauxhall Walk
London SE11 5HJ

Printed in Great Britain by
Richard Clay Ltd, Bungay, Suffolk

British Library Cataloguing in Publication Data
Hendry, Diana
Hetty's first fling.
I. Title   II. Series
823'.914[J]   PZ7
ISBN 0-7445-1419-3

Hetty's First Fling

Written by
DIANA HENDRY

Illustrated by
NICOLE GOODWIN

WALKER BOOKS
LONDON

Contents

1   The Invitation, 7

2   The Journey, 23

3   Little Chiefs and Wee Girlies, 41

4   The Party, 52

For George

1 The Invitation

The invitation to Great Uncle Fergus's party arrived at the Mungoes' squeezed-in little terrace on a Monday morning in Spring.

"He's having a party," said Mr. Mungoe in a funeral voice.

"Whatever for?" asked Mrs. Mungoe, snapping the toast out of the toaster as though the two slices were the back and front of Great Uncle Fergus who ought to be toasted alive for thinking of such a terrible thing as a party.

"Will it be on the island?" breathed Hetty, but nobody answered.

"I am not going," said James. James, aged fourteen, had not spoken for a year. Instead of words he twanged his guitar. C major meant 'yes', G major meant 'no'. They got by. Now all the family looked at him. "I am not going," he repeated. "I shall never forgive Great Uncle Fergus," and he picked up his guitar from beside his chair, where it waited like a trusty dog, and twanged C major, G major, C major, G major, one after the other. (This meant 'I am very upset'.)

"Will it be on the island?" asked Hetty again.

"We'll have to go," said Mr. Mungoe, "Uncle

Fergus is seventy-five, he's asking the whole family. He says he wants to get everyone together before he dies."

"When's he dying?" asked Hetty. Hetty was nine.

"Twang!" went James's guitar in G major. (Never.)

Mrs. Mungoe folded her hands in her lap and closed her eyes for a long time like one who has much to endure. "Off the beaten track," she moaned. "If Uncle Fergus were any more off the beaten track he'd fall into the sea. Mountain and moor and bog! Hay stacks where there should be shops! A hundred and one varieties of whisky and not a brown sliced loaf in sight." Mrs. Mungoe was a town person. When she was out in the country she had the uncomfortable feeling of the world being unmade, as if God had not yet reached this part and had simply left the raw ingredients in a bowl to be cooked into streets and houses, churches and stations, when He had time.

"I'll buy you some climbing boots," said Mr. Mungoe disappearing through the kitchen door,

9

"and a compass."

"Huh!" said Mrs. Mungoe.

"Twang!" said James's guitar. (Ha! Ha!)

For a moment Mr. Mungoe's face peered through the doorway. The gloom of his wife and son seemed to have cheered him up. He looked at Hetty sitting at the end of the table in her red dressing-gown with marmalade golly brooches marching down the lapel. "Yes," he said, "the party *will* be on the island," and he vanished.

10

Mrs. Mungoe, who disliked mornings as much as she disliked the country, hid herself behind the newspaper so that just the top of her fierce red hair – Hetty's hair – showed, and waited for James and Hetty to go away, which they soon did, James to lie on his bed and twang dark chords and Hetty to her attic to look over the London clutter of roofs and chimneys and to think about the island.

Great Uncle Fergus's island was the Isle of Skye. Hetty had never been there and she had not so much a picture-in-her-mind about it as a feeling-in-her-bones. She thought it was as wild as Great Uncle Fergus's hair and as rough as his hairy oatmeal socks which he wore with his kilt, and as cold as his cheeks which, when she kissed him, felt chilled by mountain winds. Mainly what Hetty thought about when she looked out at the crowded London roofs with their curly red tiles or polished grey slates, was all that space. The island, Hetty thought up there in her poky attic, was somewhere you could stretch and stretch and stretch, and never have to tuck your elbows in. It was somewhere

11

you could stride with big long strides like
Great Uncle Fergus took.

Hetty was the only Mungoe who liked Great
Uncle Fergus and, in truth, Hetty didn't so much
like Great Uncle as she liked to dream about his
island. Great Uncle himself was rather alarming,
Hetty thought, and so did all the Mungoes.

The trouble was that Great Uncle Fergus was
determined to be a proper Uncle. He had no
children of his own so he made up for it with
other people's, like someone who has never
been allowed puddings as a child and makes up
for it by eating ice cream ever after. Great
Uncle Fergus made endless visits to those of his
relations who had children. He didn't care for
grown-ups or for anyone under six months old,
but if you were between six months and
fourteen years, then you could be sure of a visit
from Great Uncle Fergus.

It was a pity that Great Uncle Fergus had a
dream idea about children (much as Hetty had
a dream idea about islands) and that none of his
nieces and nephews were anything like the
child of that dream.

This child, a boy, liked museums, ice-cream, Battersea fun-fair, narrow-gauge railways and Westerns more-or-less in that order and more-or-less all the things G.U.F. liked but which, on his remote island, he had little of. Worst of all was the fact that Great Uncle Fergus thought that every boy of the family would be proud to wear the tartan of the Mungoe clan. When James was ten, he had had made for him a kilt in green, blue and black tartan and had made James wear it all round town – to James's horror and the hoots of his friends. This was the deed for which James would never forgive Great Uncle Fergus.

At Christmas G.U.F. sent all the children boxes of pencils with their names printed in silver on each one, and on birthdays he sent Scottish pound notes which James changed as fast as he could at the Post Office, but which Hetty kept in a special pocket of her purse and didn't like to spend.

Once a year G.U.F. visited them on his way from the Mungoes in Chester to the Mungoes in Eastbourne so that Mrs. Mungoe said that he must live very cheaply because there was always some Mungoe or other to provide him with food, but Mr. Mungoe said this was unfair, think of the things G.U.F. bought for the children. At which James twanged a very ear-hurting chord which sounded like 'kilts'.

Great Uncle Fergus had been to see them last summer and stayed for a week. He had not mentioned a party then although he'd looked very old already. Hetty thought his scrawny neck seemed to be stretching for the sky like a giraffe's and his hair had caught the snow as the tops of mountains do. The Mungoes' small front room seemed to shrink as soon as G.U.F.'s shoulder, with its hump of knapsack, heaved through the door. Hetty felt as if a man from another world had arrived, bringing with him all that world's strange weathers. It was G.U.F.'s kilted knees that did it. Hetty sat on the pouffe in the corner and stared at them. It was easy to stare because G.U.F. never noticed Hetty. G.U.F. was only interested in the sons of the family (alas for James), his 'Little Highland Chiefs' he called them.

Great Uncle Fergus's knees were pale, bare, boney and hairless. They looked very exposed, like two bald policemen without helmets or two babies without bonnets. Bare and daring were Great Uncle's knees and around them jigged the kilt with its savage silver pin, large enough for a giant baby's nappy, only this pin had a purple stone in it the colour of heather and probably won in a battle with another Highland Chief.

Hetty imagined that there were still battles, with swords, fought in Highland glens and such big shoes as G.U.F. wore could only be for leaping down rocky hills with a whoop and a war cry.

"Well now," Great Uncle Fergus was saying to James who, bribed by three L.P.s and a set of new guitar strings, stood shiftily before him, "I see you've grown out of your kilt."

James, who had never grown *into* his kilt attempted a smile. "Hetty would love a kilt," he said. "She's never had one."

"The wee girlie?" said Great Uncle, feeling first James's calves and then what passed for

16

biceps in James's thin arms. "Ah well, her
mother can see to that. My job's to see to you
Highland Chiefs." Great Uncle always called

Hetty, 'the wee girlie'. Hetty wasn't even sure if he knew her name even though her pencils had Henrietta Mungoe printed on them very clearly in silver.

"Well, I'm not a very Highland person, Uncle . . ." James began.

"Nonsense, man!" said Great Uncle, squeezing James's frail and lowland arm. "It's in the blood. A wee bit of island porridge would soon stiffen that arm for you. Make you toss the caber!"

Neither Hetty nor James knew what a caber was and neither liked to ask; James because the answer might take half an hour and because he might be asked to toss whatever it was, and Hetty because she liked to imagine it was a Scottish chimney pot tossed in a vast frying pan like a pancake.

Great Uncle Fergus stayed for a week. He marched James round the British Museum, the Victoria and Albert Museum, the War Museum and even the Dolls' House Museum. He wouldn't hear a single twang out of the guitar and whenever James attempted the quietest

'thrum' Great Uncle shouted, "Wheesht! Hold your noise, man! If you want noise I'll buy you bagpipes!" This threat kept James musically silent for the whole week.

Great Uncle Fergus insisted on soup every day even though the weather was hot. "We always have soup on the island," said G.U.F. "Cock-a-leekie, lentil, barley, pea," and Hetty went about the house singing quietly to herself, "Cock-a-leekie, lentil, barley, pea."

Once Mrs. Mungoe said snappily that he wasn't on the island now and no-one else liked soup, or not in summer, but G.U.F. threatened to cook a haggis so after that she kept quiet although every night, when G.U.F. was snoring

19

a loud Highland snore, she said to Mr. Mungoe: "Little Highland Chiefs!" in a tone of great disgust.

Mr. Mungoe almost always made the same reply. "Well dear, he doesn't have a family of his own."

"He doesn't want one!" cried Mrs. Mungoe. "He just wants a legion of Highland Chiefs. Why he's hardly looked at our poor Hetty."

This was true. Great Uncle Fergus patted our poor Hetty's head about twice a day and said, "Here's the wee girlie." But that didn't make any difference to Hetty. She was the only one in the family who thought that Great Uncle Fergus of the brave, bare knees was a hero.

At the end of the week, G.U.F. got out the tape measure that he always kept in his pocket for measuring his Little Chiefs and measured James (arm-pit, waist, shoulder-to-waist, waist-to-knee), and wrote it all down in his little tartan book promising that James should have a brand new kilt.

After that he humped his knapsack on his back and, with his bare knees shining in the sun

20

and his white hair bright as mountains in snow,
he swung down the road to the station.

Mrs. Mungoe and James danced a jig to
celebrate and Mr. Mungoe took off the tartan
tie he'd worn all week, but Hetty stayed at the
window watching the giant figure of Great
Uncle Fergus swinging down the road. The
garters round his socks had little tartan tags
that danced like butterflies about his knees as
he walked.

Only Hetty was sad when G.U.F. left and only Hetty was glad when the invitation to Great Uncle's party arrived.

"Will there be a cake with seventy-five candles?" she asked her mother.

"There'll probably be cock-a-leekie, lentil, barley and pea soup," said Mrs. Mungoe. "And haggis."

But Hetty went off to school thinking that they would toss the caber over the mountains and catch it in a frying pan on the other side, and that she would surely have a kilt with butterflies at her knees and would run across the moor, through heather and through cotton grass and there would be so much space she'd be able to stretch and stretch and stretch until her fingers reached the very edges of the world.

2   The Journey

As it was, Hetty cried because she didn't have a kilt and James *nearly* cried because he did.

Mrs. Mungoe said women and girls weren't expected to wear kilts but men and boys were, and it cost a lot of money to get to the island and a lot of money to hire a kilt for Mr. Mungoe and Hetty had a nice blue party frock and that would have to do. Mrs. Mungoe was so cross about the party that she said she was going to wear an orange dress which, put beneath her red hair, made you go 'ouch!' It was her protest she said.

James did a lot of protesting too. Mostly in A minor and D minor and worst of all, B flat minor. He sat in his bedroom with the blind

pulled down playing the saddest chords he
knew, until Mrs. Mungoe cried into the frying
pan and the frying pan fat sizzled and spat.

Just before the party, a large parcel came for
James with a sea-blue post-mark on it saying
'Isle of Skye'. Nobody wanted to open it. It lay
on the kitchen table for two days. Now and
then Hetty rested her finger on the post-mark
as if she might soak in the sea around the Isle.

Eventually Mr. Mungoe persuaded James
down into the kitchen and they opened the
parcel. The kilt came attached to a white linen
bodice. It was blue and green and black tartan
and there was a big nappy pin with it, but the
big pin didn't have a stone in it. Hetty thought
that James was probably too little a chief to
have a stone in his kilt pin and she wondered
if all chiefs began, like James, by not wanting
to be chiefs and what became of little girls who
wanted to be chiefesses but couldn't! With the
kilt was a hairy purse on a belt that Mr.
Mungoe said was a sporran, socks, and two
garters with tartan butterfly tags. Hetty, her
thumb in her mouth, looked at them with

24

longing eyes.

James put on all his Little Chief clothes and stood before his family, his face a rhinoceros-sag of misery. "Cheer up, James," said Mr. Mungoe, "I'll let you dye your hair and put an earring in your ear when we come home!" James snarled an A minor snarl.

Hetty thought he looked wonderful. Except for his knees. James's knees were dimpled and round and friendly – not brave and bare. They were London sort of knees, squashed-up-on-the-tube sort of knees, comforted knees. Mr. Mungoe's knees weren't quite right for his kilt either. They were very pale and unsure of themselves and the hairs stuck out in a startled sort of way as if surprised to find themselves without the covering of trousers. Mrs. Mungoe laughed when she saw Mr. Mungoe's knees in the kilt and said they were more like the knees of Highland cattle than Highland chiefs. She painted her nails as red as a double-decker London bus and said this was another protest.

But Mr. Mungoe in his hired kilt that was the same tartan as James's, had cheered up a good deal and began to swagger in a way that made the pleats of his kilt swing. And then he pretended his city umbrella was a shepherd's crook and strode about the kitchen making "Hoa! Hoa!" sheep-calling noises.

They were to travel to Scotland on the overnight train. It left London at midnight and midnight, on the day of departure, seemed to Hetty as distant as the moon. James played the

blues on his guitar all day. Mr. Mungoe taught
Hetty a Scottish dance called the Gay Gordons
and whirled her about the kitchen on his arm.

In the afternoon Mrs. Mungoe showed them
the birthday present she had bought for Great
Uncle Fergus. It was an old map of the island.
They sat round the kitchen table and Mr.
Mungoe read out the names of the places –
Talisker, Carbost, Soay, Vaternish, Dunvegan,
Ullinish, Portnalong, Portree, Torvaig. The
'ishy' names reminded Hetty of the wind or a

lullaby. Her eyelids drooped. "You can have a
sleep," said Mr. Mungoe as Hetty's thumb went
in, "you'll be up very late for the midnight
train," and he carried Hetty upstairs.

When she woke up it was dusk. She looked
out of the window at the low, smoky London
sky. On the island the sky would be much
higher than it was here. In fact that must be
why it was called Skye – because there was
more sky there than anywhere else – and there
would be a space as big as Hyde Park in which
to dance the Highland Fling and toss the
chimney pot.

Hours and hours after the street lamps had
come on and the first stars could be seen above
the roofs, the taxi came for them. The West
End flashed all its lights as they rattled past,
Trafalgar Square tossed down its fountains like
bouquets of rain-drops, other taxis honked
goodbye to them.

At the last minute, when they reached the
station and got out of the taxi, they realised
that James had somehow smuggled in his guitar
wrapped up in his anorak. For a moment Mr.

Mungoe looked as if he might explode and his eyebrows stuck out like toothbrush bristles, but then Mrs. Mungoe produced, from her pocket, her very special vegetable peeling knife

(without which she was not at home anywhere), and Hetty produced Panda who should have been in her suitcase but wasn't because he would have suffocated there and anyway, he wanted to see what was going on. Mr. Mungoe viewed all these treasures and threw up his hands and said, "What a family!" and marched them all onto the platform.

The midnight sleeper was already waiting for

them, its helmeted head like a silver submarine
of the night. Mr. Mungoe had reserved two
compartments. Hetty thought they were like
little cabins on a ship. James climbed up to the
top bunk and lay there, his thumb in his
mouth (although, of course, he was far too old
for this) and his guitar cuddled to his chest.

"Not a C major out of you tonight," Mr. Mungoe had said, so James just lay there, patting the guitar strings in a 'there, there' kind of way. But Hetty, wide awake, explored every inch of the cabin.

Mrs. Mungoe helped Hetty to wash and to put on her pyjamas. "All aboard, sailor," she said and Hetty climbed in. There was just room for Panda.

There was a very small shelf on the wall beside Hetty and Hetty said it was a pity to leave the shelf empty and Mrs. Mungoe said yes, if there was one thing she couldn't abide it was an empty shelf. But it was too little for a book (which might fall down when the train was going) and it was just the right size for specs (if you wore specs, but Hetty didn't), so they settled for a handkerchief; and the shelf looked much better when it was full of handkerchief, and Hetty snuggled down to wait for the train to start.

Then Mrs. Mungoe, with her red hair falling out of its pins, stood with her hands on her hips and looked up at James on the top bunk (with one thumb in his mouth and one arm round the dead body of his guitar) and Mrs. Mungoe said, "When all this is over, James, I shall buy you six guitar lessons and another set

of new strings." James did not want to look too happy too soon, so he took his thumb out slowly and climbed down the ladder and said maybe he'd put his pyjamas on now. And by the time Mr. Mungoe came in to give them a goodnight kiss, they were both tucked in their bunks and James had a packet of chewing gum on *his* shelf and the guitar slept on the lid of the wash-basin with its mouth wide open.

Soon there was a banging of doors, shouts, a long whistle, a terrific jerk as if the sleeper had indeed been asleep and had woken up with a terrible start, and they were off, creaking and unsteady at first and then gathering speed and a regular rhythm as though a music teacher with a baton were out in front saying, "Now, *one* two three four, *one* two three four – keep time!" And the train did and Hetty and James – who at first thought they would never sleep with such a noise – soon did.

When Hetty woke up, the train seemed to be riding very lightly along the tracks and James was up at the window, still in his pyjamas. The blind was up and as Hetty looked out she saw

first brown, craggy rocks going up, up, up and
then, to her astonishment, a deer, its antlers —
large and knobbly as the coat-hooks in James's
school cloakroom — set very wide and surprised
and shaping a huge grin on the face of the hills.
There were more of them as Hetty joined James

at the window and each one stood and stared at the sleeper train with that strange, quiet stare of animals who own the land.

At Inverness they left the sleeper, and caught a small two-coach train to Kyle. And then came the ferry.

Chubby as a baby's bath boat, it had a bright red funnel, a shining brass rail and its name was 'The Bonnie Prince Charlie'. Mr. Mungoe told Hetty that he was the most famous Highland Chief of all and that he'd loved a girl from the island called Flora Macdonald.

Sea-gulls clung about the funnel of the ferry like fans about a pop-star until a policeman of a wind blew them, crying, away. James and Hetty put on their cagoules and scarves and found a whitewashed bench on deck. They all huddled together. The funnel made a noise like a polite gentleman coughing and then a rather ruder gentleman belching and then, as if it could not wait a moment longer, it gave a great hoot at the sky and they were at sea.

After about ten minutes on the choppy waters James and Mrs. Mungoe began to feel a

bit odd. Mrs. Mungoe turned so pale that her freckles stood out like stars on a dark night and James went the colour of old parsnips. They said they would go below so that they wouldn't feel the boat rocking so much. Hetty and Mr. Mungoe snuggled together and Hetty watched a man at the prow who was wearing a kilt and whose butterfly tags fluttered very fast in the wind. Mr. Mungoe sang 'Over the sea to Skye' in a low, deep voice and Hetty said, "I wish I could be a Little Highland Chief and have butterflies at my knees," and Mr. Mungoe gave her an extra hug.

Then all too quickly they were there and the sailors were tossing out the ropes to other sailors who were waiting for them and who wound them round big iron cotton reels. There on the dock with his kilt and his white hair was Great Uncle Fergus, not looking quite so much a giant out here where there really *was* a lot of space, as he looked in London, but still, with his straight back and his hairy jacket and his hairy socks (and the brave warrior knees) looking very much a Chief. Because it was his birthday he was wearing a sprig of heather in his button-hole.

Hetty, suddenly not caring whether G.U.F. only saw her as 'that wee girlie', took out her blue spotted handkerchief and waved it like mad. And G.U.F. grinned and took out his, (striped) and waved it back. Then they all

lurched and staggered down the gang-plank calling "Happy Birthday! Happy Birthday!" (Mrs. Mungoe and James rather quietly because their tummies were not yet back in their proper places.)

"Well, how's my Little Highland Chief?" asked G.U.F. ignoring everyone else and clapping James on the shoulder so that James's tummy fell two inches at once. Without waiting for a reply he turned to the others. "Well then clan, ready for the ceilidh?"

"What's a ceilidh?" whispered Hetty to her father.

"A party," Mr. Mungoe whispered back and Hetty's heart went soaring like a sea-gull into the high, high, island sky.

3 Little Chiefs and Wee Girlies

Great Uncle Fergus lived in one of the places with a wind-whispering name. Talisker. He drove them down the narrow island road and Hetty saw the moors full of blue scabias and cotton grass and here and there a small croft crouched low under the big sky, each with a tin shack painted scarlet or yellow at its side. Many of the crofts had a large yellow bun of hay held against the wind by a fishing net. Some of the houses were thatched and the thatch was tied down with ropes and the ropes weighted with stones. There was enough sky and wind here for a roof to blow 'whoops' and away.

Sometimes they passed trenches dug in the

41

bog by the islanders for the peat which they used for their fires and which smelt like brewing tea. The slices of dark brown soggy peat were laid along the trenches to dry and looked like enormous slabs of treacle toffee. Hetty looked everywhere to see if she could see someone tossing a chimney pot but she couldn't. The road was so narrow that when another car came the other way G.U.F. had to pull into a lay-by and wait for it to pass. But of course what was nicest of all about the island was that the sea was so close all around you. It held you in a hug and you always knew where you were because you stood within its arms.

G.U.F. turned off down a bumpy road that made Mrs. Mungoe groan and say that *this* must be what was meant by 'going off the beaten track'. And by the time they'd bumped to the bottom of the track to G.U.F.'s tall stone house,

all the pins had fallen out of her hair and Mr.
Mungoe said she looked like a red-haired
scarecrow.

To the surprise of James and Hetty, G.U.F.'s
house was a hundred yards from the beach of
Talisker Bay. In all his talk about the island
G.U.F. had never mentioned this. Probably the
beach at the bottom of his garden was as
commonplace to him as the bus stop at the
bottom of James's and Hetty's.

James and Hetty were all for ignoring the
house – big and grand though it seemed – and
running straight to the beach, but G.U.F. held
them back. "Unpack first," he said, "then all
my Little Highland Chiefs can spend the

afternoon on the beach while we grown-ups get ready for the ceilidh.''

"*And* the wee girlies!'' piped Hetty. G.U.F. gave her an odd look and said, "Yes, *and* the wee girlies.''

So they went into the house which had big grey flags on the floor and pictures of Highland Chiefs everywhere and a big goat's head over the stairs, only Mr. Mungoe said it wasn't a goat it was an ibex. Hetty found she was in a bedroom with five other girls and that these 'wee girlies' were all her cousins. (James, as one of seven Little Highland Chiefs, had a room to himself – the house was that big.)

All the 'wee girlies' were ranged on the sides of their beds looking gloomy. "Well,'' said the largest of them who was fuzzing her hair out with a spikey brush, "*we* don't matter, do we? It's the precious little Highland Chiefs who matter.''

"I *won't* sing Happy Birthday, I won't!'' said a second wee girlie.

"I'll put a spider in his sporran!'' said a third scraggy cousin with a brace on her teeth.

44

"I'll shove oat cakes down his socks!" said a fourth.

"I'll blow out all his candles!" said the fifth.

"And I won't toss the chimney pot!" cried Hetty, not wanting to be left out. There was a silence after this and Hetty was sorry she had spoken because although G.U.F. didn't seem to care for Hetty, Hetty cared for G.U.F.

Things were little better among the seven Little Highland Chiefs. Only one of them, Robin, lived on the island, the rest didn't even live in Scotland and none of them wanted to wear a kilt or be a Highland Chief. They wanted jeans and discos and guitars and motor-bikes. They ganged together on the beach that afternoon, sitting round an old crate set on the black sand, and looking like a plot of pirates hunched over the treasure-map of their miseries.

Indeed it was a very pirate-like beach, surrounded by cliffs and with a wind so strong that the thirty-foot water-fall blew upwards, as if they were in a strange magic land where water-falls blew upwards and white sand became black. The beach was littered with the

bones of lost sheep, boxes with foreign names burnt on their sides, crates and orange and blue ropes from ships which Hetty felt sure had been wrecked there. Above the cliffs hooded crows waged war on four buzzards.

Only Robin wandered off to watch the battle, climbing easily over the rocks with his binoculars hung round his neck. He moved with the freedom of a boy who has always known a lot of space. Hetty thought he made all the other boys look cramped in their clothes. Robin wore his kilt as easily as James wore jeans.

Once Robin clambered down to where Hetty was writing on the sand with the tip of a gull's

feather. He stood over her, watching, a tall,
serious boy with a face that expected surprises.

"Yesterday I saw the death cart," he said
abruptly.

HAPPY BIRTH, wrote Hetty in the sand.

"It's all black," said Robin, "and when you

see it, it means someone's going to die."

"Great Uncle Fergus?" asked Hetty, alarmed. Robin shrugged. "Who knows?" he said mysteriously. "It might be me, it might be you, it might be anyone."

DAY GREAT UNCLE, Hetty continued determinedly, as though writing it might make sure it *wasn't* Great Uncle Fergus who got carried away in the death cart.

"Do you believe in fairies?" Robin asked, just as abruptly. Hetty hesitated. James, she knew, would sneer at fairies and so would all her friends. But Robin was somehow different. His mind wasn't tied down with ropes and stones like the thatched roofs. Wind and sky had blown into it. Wind and sky, dreams and fairies, buzzards and crows and death carts.

"Well, yes I do," said Hetty. "Do you?"

"Oh yes," said Robin easily, "I've seen them."

FERGUS, wrote Hetty with triumph. But before she had time to ask any more questions Great Uncle Fergus himself appeared, standing on a rock near the house and banging a loud brass gong. It was time to go in.

Somehow the gong was like raw excitement sent straight to their party spirits. But the Little Chiefs were not to be won so easily. They slouched into the house, their hands in their pockets. The girls who, for a brief hour, had become Joanne, Charlotte, Alice, Julia and Marie, remembered that they were nameless wee girlies again and lost their smiles.

If it hadn't been for the swing of Robin's kilt and the brightness of Hetty's eyes, you would never have guessed that Great Uncle Fergus's amazing Highland party was about to begin.

4 The Party

It was said that on the night of Great Uncle
Fergus's party the lights from his house could
be seen in Portree and the noise of bagpipes and
fiddles could be heard on the mainland.

Everyone came. The whole clan. There was
G.U.F.'s important brother, The Hon. Alexander
Ian Lachlan Mungoe M.P. – known as The
Eagle of the North. There were three nephews
who came all the way from their sheep farm in
Australia in their woolly jerseys. There were
forty-five cousins who were once removed and
twice removed and thrice removed and more
times removed than anyone could ever work
out. There was Aunt Euphemia who had not
been beyond her front door since 1965 and who

came in a purple Rolls Royce with a hot water-bottle tied round her middle. There was Murdo Mungoe the sailor, and Mungo Mungoe the vet, and Aunt Morag Agnes Mungoe whose dangling earrings nearly touched the floor.

When the gang of Little Chiefs came down in their kilts (looking like prisoners of war), and the wee girlies came down (pretty on the outside and snarling on the in), they found the doors of the main rooms flung open and they all opened their mouths wide and said, "Oooooooh!"

Great Uncle Fergus had hired disco lights. The room moved with all the colours of a paint-box. It was like walking on a planet where multi-coloured moons swam around you. In one room a table as long as the clan itself was draped with Scottish flags and set in the centre was a great silver tureen of raspberry ice-cream chilled by small ice-bergs. On the right was the cake, all seventy-five layers of it, like a sand-wich for a giant, with chocolate butter icing oozing out of the sides of it and seventy-five candles crowded on the top of it. On the left

was an enormous purple jelly, the colour of Aunt Euphemia's Rolls Royce, moulded into the shape of the Loch Ness Monster.

In the moon room, as Hetty called it to herself, the bagpipers and fiddlers took it in turn to play The Strathspey Reel and The Duke of Perth and, between two crossed swords, The Hon. Alexander danced a neat and nimble sword dance.

No-one, until that night, had guessed that Great Uncle Fergus was so good at giving parties. He was good at giving them because his life on the island, with its long, dark winters, was such a quiet one that when he *did* have a party, he wanted it to be the loudest, brightest, biggest, *Chiefest* party ever known. And it was.

Everyone danced and drank and ate Loch Ness Monster Jelly and Ice-Berg Ice-cream and greeted their long lost cousins – four-times-removed and Hetty danced a Foursome Reel with Murdo and Mungo and Morag and the Dashing White Seargent with Robin. Robin cupped his hands round her ear and above the noise of the bag-pipes shouted, "There's still a surprise to come!"

But despite all this fun, everyone was still a bit afraid of Great Uncle Fergus. Maybe it was because he was bigger than anyone else and his clothes were prickly and so was his temper. Whatever it was, when G.U.F. banged his golden gong as though he rang the northern star and said, "Ladies and Gentlemen, it is time for the Gay Gordons – which of you fine ladies will be my partner?" there was a sudden silence. The fiddlers held their bows against their fiddles, the bagpipers rested their elbows on their bags. Mr. Mungoe pinched Mrs. Mungoe but she pretended not to notice.

Then Hetty could bear it no longer. She
marched across the multi-coloured moon room
in her Skye-blue party dress and said, "I'll be
your partner, Great Uncle Fergus." And Great
Uncle Fergus said, "Who are you?" because he
couldn't tell one wee girlie from another, they
were all just names on pencils to him. Hetty
said very firmly, "I am Hetty," and G.U.F. said,
"Hetty! Oh yes, you waved your spotty hankie
to me." Then everyone laughed and clapped

and made up a set for the Gay Gordons and in between swopping partners and whirling round and round, Hetty managed to tell Great Uncle Fergus how much she'd wanted a kilt (and particularly the butterfly bits round the socks), and how she'd wanted to dance the Gay Gordons out in the open so that she could stretch and stretch and stretch and not have to tuck her elbows in. And G.U.F. told her she was a funny wee girlie and Hetty reminded him that her name was Hetty.

By then it was nearly midnight and G.U.F. banged the gong again and told them that there was one last surprise (Robin winked at Hetty) and they were all to go down to the beach. When they got there they saw a huge bonfire, tall as the waterfall, blazing up to the high Skye sky.

The fiddlers came down to the beach too, struggling with their music against roar of water and crackle of flame. Before they began to play, Great Uncle Fergus climbed onto a rock and said, "Now clan, we are going to dance the Gay Gordons one more time – and this time especially for Hetty!" Then he got off his rock, walked over to Hetty, bowed and said "May I have the pleasure?" And Hetty said, "Delighted," which she thought was the proper thing to say. Then the Little Chiefs – who had been having such a good time they'd forgotten they were wearing kilts – and the wee girlies – now pretty inside and out – stripped off their shoes and socks and all the grown-ups followed their example, and they all danced the Gay

Gordons on the beach in flame light and wave
light to the faint, fairy-like sound of the
fiddles.

Hetty swung from partner to partner with
all the space in the world to dance in. Once she

whirled round with her arm crooked in Robin's
who went so fast that Hetty got dizzy and
thought her feet might leave the sand and fly
her to the top of the waterfall.

When that was over they all joined hands
round the bonfire and sang 'Happy Birthday'
at the tops of their voices. While they were
doing this, Aunt Morag and Aunt Euphemia
turned the lights of the house off and lit the
candles on the cake so that when they went
inside they were all hushed by the sudden,
silent delight of so many candles.

But Great Uncle Fergus cried, "This is a
party!" and switched the disco lights on again
and cut the seventy-five layered cake into
hundreds of slices (Uncle Murdo had five and
Mungo had sixteen), so that by the time they
all fell into bed at the end of the party, there
wasn't a lick of chocolate butter icing left.

The next morning, while everyone else was
still asleep, Hetty looked out of her window and
saw Robin herding the cows to the top of the
hill. She crept out of bed and down the stairs.
The house looked as topsy-turvy as if a horde

of elfin shoe-makers had been working there all night. Outside, in the brisk morning air, the world looked suddenly sensible and everydayish, as if there had never been a party with Loch Ness Monster jelly and a room full of coloured moons. Hetty went to sit on a gate which turned out to be an old brass bed-head. Perhaps the world wasn't so everydayish after all.

Soon the vet and his assistant arrived in a land-rover and Robin came to sit beside Hetty on the bed-head gate.

"He's come to give the cows an injection," said Robin. "It keeps their milk pure."

Hetty studied Robin's bare, brave knees.

"Could you show me the fairies?" she said at last.

"I couldn't do that," said Robin. "Fairies are something you see for yourself or you don't see at all."

Hetty said nothing but two tears plopped onto her own bare, brave knees. "Oh," said Robin, "you mustn't cry about it. I expect you will see them one day. You're the type."

"Really?" said Hetty.

"Oh aye," said Robin comfortably. "Tell you what though, I'll give you my butterfly tags. Great Uncle told me you'd taken a fancy to them." And Robin lifted the tops of his socks and pulled off his garters and gave them to Hetty. They were too big for her legs so she put them on the tops of her arms and went running back to the house with the butterfly tags flying in the wind.

The next day the Mungoes took the ferry home and Mr. Mungoe and Mrs. Mungoe and James all said that Great Uncle Fergus's

Seventy-fifth Birthday Party was something they would never forget. Hetty said nothing, but she waved her blue spotty handkerchief as if it was the Scottish flag itself, at G.U.F. and at Robin who came with him and whose socks had fallen down to his ankles because he had no garters.

Three weeks later a parcel arrived at the Mungoes' squeezed-in little terrace. It was addressed to Hetty. And inside was a kilt in blue, green and black tartan. *And* hairy socks. *And* garters with tartan butterfly tags. And this time they fitted.

There was a message too. It said, 'To Hetty of the high heart' and underneath, in bold, black writing, 'with love from Great Uncle Fergus, Chief !'

Diana Hendry was a journalist for several years and now teaches English at Clifton College in Bristol. She is a poet and the author of several Blackbirds and Redwings for Julia MacRae Books, including *Fiona Finds Her Tongue* (which was shortlisted for the Smarties Prize), *Midnight Pirate*, *The Not-Anywhere House*, *The Rainbow Watchers* and *The Carey Street Cat*. Her first picture book, *Christmas in Exeter Street*, was published last year also by Julia MacRae Books.

Here are some more WALKER STORYBOOK titles for you to enjoy

Our Horrible Friend

by Hannah Cole
(black and white illustrations by Julie Stiles)

Like Diane and
Jenny, Poppy lives
with her mum and
visits her dad
on Saturdays.

But when Poppy and her mum start

visiting Diane and
Jenny's dad on
Saturdays, the
two sisters are
not at all pleased.
And this is just
the first of
several surprises...

ROBIN HOOD
and *LITTLE JOHN*

by Julian Atterton
(black and white illustrations by
John Dillow)

One day, when walking
in the forest, Robin
Hood encounters a
huge stranger – and
ends up in the river!
The man is, of course,
Little John and he and Robin
soon become the best of
friends. But Little John
brings with him a
problem – a dangerous
challenge for Robin
and his men...

A WALKER STORYBOOK

STAPLES
FOR
AMOS

by Alison Morgan

(black and white illustrations
by Charles Front)

When Mum forgets to
buy staples for Amos
to mend the fence of the
bullock field, Daley acts quickly to try
and save her from the
anger of the old farm
worker. But his action
leads him into danger...

"A story of courage and determination...
A simple, imaginative and rather
moving tale."
British Book News

A WALKER STORYBOOK

EARTHQUAKE

by Ruskin Bond

(black and white illustrations by
Valerie Littlewood)

"What do you do when there's
an earthquake?" asks Rakesh.
Everyone in the Burman
household has their own
ideas, but when the tremors
begin and everything starts to shake and
quake, to crack and
crumble, they are
taken by surprise...

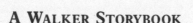

A WALKER STORYBOOK

Walker Books also publishes a range of entertaining novels by top authors. The stories cover a variety of subjects and situations – historical, adventure, suspense, horror, sci-fi, comedy and lots more. You'll find more information on some of these novels over the page.

SOMETHING RARE AND SPECIAL

Judy Allen

Following her parents' divorce, Lyn has to move out of London with her mother to a temporary home on the coast. At first, missing her old friends and city life, Lyn feels like a fish out of water in this bleak, empty landscape, but then she discovers Bill Walker and his binoculars – and something very special...

This is a beautifully written and atmospheric story by the winner of the 1988 Whitbread Children's Book Award.

"A sensitive story, rich with thoughtful atmosphere."
Junior Education

ANANCY-SPIDERMAN

James Berry

Anancy, the hero of these twenty lively and intriguing Afro-Caribbean folk tales, is both man and spider. Seemingly defenceless, he is an artful rogue who uses his cunning to outwit his opponents – the mighty Bro Tiger in particular. But these are just two in a colourful cast of characters which includes Bro Dog, Bro Monkey, Old Higue Dry-Skull, Swing-Swing Janey and many, many more.

"James Berry retells these vivid stories … in a soft, mellifluous voice that captures the magic and trickery of the spider hero."
Julia Eccleshare, Children's Books of the Year

A FEW FAIR DAYS

Jane Gardam

Enter the weird and wonderful world of Lucy's childhood. Meet Aunt Fanny, Auntie Bea and Aunt Kitty (who never stopped travelling). Discover for yourself Jinnie Love's Fair Days, nanny-nuns, akkerbeests, polycarps and queeds. Marvel over the stories of Mr Crossley's wig, the great ship, the magus Zoroaster and the beast in the mire...But, above all, prepare to be thoroughly entertained!

"Jane Gardam writes beautifully both for children and adults...An enchanting book."
The Lady

"A modern classic...It's a very evocative book."
BBC Radio

THE ARPINO ASSIGNMENT

Geoffrey Trease

It's 1943. One moment young Private Rick Weston is peeling spuds, and the next he's parachuting into occupied Italy on a vital and dangerous assignment, organized by the top secret Special Operations Executive. His mission? To find and assist the Resistance in their fight against the Nazis...

"Stirring, romantic and highly entertaining... A splendid piece of story-telling."
Leon Garfield, TES